This book belongs to:

....

OXFORD
UNIVERSITY PRESS

Great Clarendon Street, Oxford OX2 6DP

Oxford University Press is a department of the University of Oxford.
It furthers the University's objective of excellence in research, scholarship, and education by publishing worldwide.
Oxford is a registered trade mark of Oxford University Press in the UK and in certain other countries

First published 2014

British Library Cataloguing in Publication Data
Data available

ISBN: 978-0-19-273690-1 (hardback with CD)
ISBN: 978-0-19-273991-9 (hardback)
ISBN: 978-0-19-273896-7 (eBook)

1 2 3 4 5 6 7 8 9 10

for
Everyone

Printed in China

Paper used in the production of this book is a natural, recyclable product
made from wood grown in sustainable forests.
The manufacturing process conforms to the environmental regulations
of the country of origin.

**The drawings in this book were created using pencil, calligraphy
ink, wax crayon, and chalk pastel. They were collaged and coloured
using QuarkXPress and Photoshop.**

**Thank you to everyone at OUP for their enthusiasm and support
for this project, especially Peter Marley and Harriet Rogers.**

tim hopgood

WHAT A WONDERFUL WORLD

Based on the song by Bob Thiele &
George David Weiss

OXFORD
UNIVERSITY PRESS

I see **trees** of **green.**

Red roses too.

I see them bloom
for me and you.

And I think to myself . . .

What a
WONDERFUL
world.

I see skies of blue . . .

and clouds of white.

The bright blessed day . . .

the dark
sacred
night.

And I think to myself . . .

What a
WONDERFUL
world.

The colours of the rainbow, so pretty in the sky . . .

**are also on the faces
of people going by.**

I see friends shaking hands, saying,

'**How do you do?**'

They're really saying,

'I love

you!'

I hear babies cry.
I watch them grow.

They'll learn much more
than I'll ever know.

And I think to myself . . .

What a
WONDERFUL
world.

Yes, I think to myself . . .

What a
WONDERFUL
world.

What a Wonderful World
was recorded in 1967
by Louis Armstrong
Directed by Tommy Goodman
Produced by Bob Thiele

The recording was inducted into the
Grammy Hall of Fame in 1999

What a Wonderful World
by Bob Thiele and George David Weiss

I see trees of green, red roses too.
I see them bloom for me and you.
And I think to myself,
What a wonderful world.

I see skies of blue and clouds of white.
The bright blessed day; the dark sacred night.
And I think to myself,
What a wonderful world.

The colours of the rainbow, so pretty in the sky,
Are also on the faces of people going by.
I see friends shaking hands, saying,
'How do you do?'
They're really saying, 'I love you'.

I hear babies cry. I watch them grow.
They'll learn much more than I'll ever know.
And I think to myself,
What a wonderful world.

Yes, I think to myself,
What a wonderful world.

I was six years old when I first heard Louis Armstrong's recording of **What a Wonderful World**. We learnt to sing the song at school, and the lyrics made a huge impression on me. It's a song full-to-the-brim with hope and optimism and I think that's what gives it such a timeless quality. A few years ago my daughter found a recording of the song in a flea market, and gave it to me as a present. As soon as I heard Louis Armstrong's gravelly voice sing the first few lines I knew I wanted to capture the joy of the song in a picture book.

timhopgood